Running Wilde

Read more about the Wilde Family in ...

Wilde Day Out
Wilde Style
Wilde Child
Wilde Ride
Wilde Party

Other series by Jenny Oldfield:

Definitely Daisy
Totally Tom
Horses of Half-Moon Ranch
My Little Life
Home Farm Twins
The Dreamseeker Trilogy

The WILDE FAMILY

Running Wilde

by Jenny Oldfield

illustrated by Sarah Nayler

Hodder Children's Books
a division of Hodder Headline Limited

Thanks to all the *wild* kids who have told me jokes and funny stories during my visits to schools and libraries

First published in Great Britain in 2003
by Hodder Children's Books

10 9 8 7 6 5 4 3 2 1

A Catalogue record for this book is available from the British Library.

ISBN 0 340 87320 5

Printed and bound in Great Britain by Bookmarque Ltd, Croydon

The paper and board used in this paperback by Hodder Children's Books are natural recyclable products made from wood grown in sustainable forests. The manufacturing processes conform to the environmental regulations of the country of origin.

Hodder Children's Books
a division of Hodder Headline Ltd
338 Euston Road
London NW1 3BH

One

Beh-doing, beh-doing! Deanne Wilde jumped along the pavement ahead of Jade and Kayleigh.

'Which d'you like best, the Ice-blue or the Wicked Lady Purple?' Kayleigh asked, showing Jade two different colours of nail varnish.

Jade hopscotched down the paving slabs. 'Dunno. Don't care.'

Beh-doing! Deanne bounced towards a doddery old lady with a pull-along shopping bag on wheels.

'She thinks she's a kangaroo,' Kayleigh explained, very matter of fact.

The woman gave Deanne a wide berth. Deanne did her Skippy impression, a rope tied around her waist and trailing behind, hands tucked under her chin like paws. She leaped along like crazy.

'Watch it!' Jade yelled as their youngest sister reached a traffic light. She sprinted ahead to press the green-man button. 'Hang on,' she gasped. 'What's your hurry?'

Deanne snuffled the air. 'Forest fire!' she said in a squeaky kangaroo-type voice. 'Gotta get out of here!'

'Purple?' Kayleigh sauntered along, lifting first one hand then the other to inspect her fingernails. 'Or blue?'

The green man flashed on and Deanne hopped across the road, trailing her rope tail. *Beh-doing!*

'Blue? Or purple?' *Oops!* Kayleigh had missed the green man. Now she would be mega-late for picking up Kyle from playgroup.

Outside the Fish Dish, Deanne and

Jade stood waiting. The smell of chips frying in the big metal frier made their mouths water.

'Yum!' Deanne sighed.

'Kangaroos don't eat fish and chips,' Jade reminded her.

'C'mon, you two!' Kayleigh bossed, as finally she made it across the road. Catching sight of herself in the Fish Dish window, she paused to fix the pale lilac beads in her long brown hair. 'These stupid things keep slipping down!' she muttered. She rearranged them, then smoothed her frilly lilac top and tightened the belt on her cut-off jeans.

'Whoo-ooh, Ms Supermodel!' Jade scoffed.

Kayleigh whacked her on the bum.

'Fire!' Skippy squeaked, bounding ahead again.

Jules was waiting with Kyle at the door to the Kangaroo Club.

'Sorry we're late,' Kayleigh gasped, taking the toddler from the playgroup leader's arms.

'You're the last ones to pick up – again!' Jules said severely. She looked frazzled after a morning spent splitting up squabbles and mopping up tears.

'Yeah, we're sorry. Gran didn't realize.'

Grubby Kyle grabbed Kayleigh's beads and tugged hard. 'Ouch!' Kayleigh yelped. 'She was cooking lunch and didn't notice the time.'

'I bet she'll be glad when your mum and dad get back,' Jules sighed. Gran Wilde had sent Kyle to playgroup with odd socks and shoes, pink trousers that were too big and a nappy on backwards. The poor boy had looked like he hadn't slept much the night before and had been wearing most of his breakfast on his striped T-shirt.

'No, she likes looking after us!' Jade assured her, sneaking into the playgroup behind Jules's back.

'Tell her that Kyle needs an afternoon nap,' Jules advised Kayleigh.

Beh-doing! Deanne hopped up to the life-size painted kangaroo that advertized the Kangaroo Club. She snuffled and squeaked with excitement.

'She thinks she's a kangaroo,' Kayleigh explained. *How many times was that?*

('They're off their trollies, the lot of them!' Jules said later to her husband.)

'Where's Jade got to?' she demanded, turning and marching inside. Sally, the Kangaroo Club helper, was busy putting away equipment and cleaning up spilt orange juice. 'Have you seen Jade Wilde?' Jules asked.

'Yeah, she's here somewhere.' Sally replied.

'Where?' Jules looked around the wreckage of plastic tractors, finger-paints, building-bricks and biscuit crumbs.

'Try the ball pool,' Sally suggested.

Wicked! Jade was perched at the top of the bright yellow slide, looking down at a sea of coloured balls. She hadn't tried this since she was three and a fully joined-up member of the Kangaroo Club herself. True, the slide looked titchy now, but it was still a good laugh.

Whizz! Whee! Jade launched herself and landed with a squish and a squirm of plastic balls. Then she faked swimming

the front crawl to the side of the pool.

'Jade Wilde, how old are you?' Jules demanded as Jade surfaced. She stood with her hands on her hips, frowning but trying not to smile.

('That Jade is hyper-active!' she told her husband. 'And you remember me telling you about Kayleigh way back? She's turned into a right little madam. Deanne's – well, Deanne's still Deanne!')

'I'm nine!' Jade confessed, sighing as she clambered out of the ball pool.

'Nine going on two!' Jules retorted.

Jade stood up tall and proud in her blue shorts, red T-shirt and trainers. 'I'm in the school swimming team!' she told her old playgroup leader proudly. 'I'm going in for my bronze life-saving medal next term!'

'Grub, glorious grub!' Carmel munched her way through a fat, juicy burger and a mountain of chips. It was the weekend; one whole week with Gran already and another week still to go.

'Don't eat with your mouth open,' her twin, Krystal, warned her. 'People will stare.'

'Huh?' Carmel paused mid-chew. 'If I don't open my mouth, how am I supposed to get my food in?'

'You know what I mean! Look at that man over there. He thinks you're disgusting!'

Chomp-chomp. Carmel stabbed another forkful of fries and stuffed them in. 'He's staring because he thinks he's seeing double,' she commented. 'And that's without drinking his usual five pints of beer!'

'Pass the ketchup, Carmel dear,' Gran said to Krystal.

'I'm Krystal,' Krystal said, though she knew it wouldn't make any difference.

'Krystal, eat with your mouth closed,' Gran told Carmel, who sniggered.

The whole Wilde family had come for a Saturday treat to have lunch at the

Snail and Cucumber. Or was it the Slug and Lettuce? Anyway, it was a place that served wicked burgers and gave you fizzy pop in a paper cup the size of a small bucket.

'I think we deserve to eat out today!' Gran had announced as she sipped coffee on the lawn at the back of the house. 'After all, Mum and Dad are off on their jollies, aren't they? Why shouldn't we have some fun as well?'

'Yeah!' Kayleigh would've killed to have been able to jet off to a sizzling hot Greek island with them. She would have got her legs mega brown for the rest of the summer and worn teenie-weenie shorts and a bare midriff.

'Yeah!' Krystal and Carmel, Jade and Deanne had echoed. Kyle had been too busy eating worms to join in.

'Where shall we go?' Gran had asked. 'I know a nice little French restaurant overlooking the market square.'

'Macdonalds!'

'Burger King!'

'Kidz R Us!'

So they'd ended up here at the Slob and Tortoise because it had a Kidz R Us play room attached.

'Finished!' Jade gulped the last mouthful of Coke and sprang to her feet. 'Can I go and play?'

'Why not sit quietly and let your food go down?' Gran asked, playing airplanes with Kyle's chips to get him to open his mouth. 'Neeyah-vroom!'

Jade fizzed like a firework. 'I don't need to,' she insisted.

'Neither do I!' Deanne jumped up and started to whinny.

'Today she's a horse,' Kayleigh explained with a sigh.

'Neigh! Brrrugh! Nei-eigh!'

'Oh all right, off you go.' Gran gave up on Kyle and began to eat his fries for him. 'I know I shouldn't!' she sighed, patting her round tummy.

'Cool!' Jade vaulted the bench and

sprinted for the games room, followed at a prancing trot by Deanne.

'Betcha I can make my drink last longer than yours!' Carmel challenged Krystal and Kayleigh, stirring the ice cubes with her straw.

'Not playing,' Krystal muttered. She made a loud, hollow sucking noise to show that she had already finished.

'Gran, do we *have* to walk back?' Kayleigh wheedled. It was a whole half mile and her legs ached already from the walk there. 'Can't we get the bus?'

Gran polished off Kyle's chips. 'The exercise will do us good.'

'Waaagh!' Kyle cried when he saw his empty plate.

The staring man leaned across his table and whispered to his wife.

'Gran, you know you shouldn't mention the word "exercise" to Kayleigh.' Krystal crunched an ice cube between her teeth.

'Yeah, she's allergenic to it,' Carmel agreed.

'Allergic.'

'Yeah, allergenic.'

Krystal giggled and spat out chunks of ice. 'Kayleigh thinks brushing her teeth is an extreme sport!'

'I don't!' Kayleigh snapped.

'Yeah, she does!' Carmel snorted. 'She skives off netball and cadges lifts wherever she goes.'

Gran picked Kyle out of his high chair and joggled him. 'There-there,

Kyley-wiley! I don't know what they're talking about on the TV when they mention these extreme sports,' she said above the row of his crying. 'In my day people did sensible things like hiking and playing cricket.'

'Yeah, but snowboarding's better,' Krystal insisted, taking Kyle from Gran and joggling him some more.

'Or paragliding, or gorge-walking, or pot-holing, or climbing Mount Kiliman-thingy!' Carmel added. *Joggle-joggle*; she took Kyle from Krystal.

'Waagh!' Kyle roared.

'Jade wants to be a surfer when she grows up.' Krystal led the way out of the restaurant into the play section. Giant cut-out clowns made an arch over the entrance into a huge room full of climbing-frames, slides, swings and a massive ball pool.

'Or a Formula One racing driver,' Carmel said, staring back at Staring Man. She ran with Kyle under the clown arch and dived into the ball pool.

Kyle came up to the surface with a surprised expression. 'Waaa-aaagh!' he said.

Then Deanne trotted past, tossing her mane from her eyes.

'Watch out!' Jade cried from the top of the slide. *Whee!* She whizzed deep into the pool and surfaced with a blue ball in her mouth.

'Waa ... !' Kyle stopped roaring and began to gurgle. He stretched out his arms for Jade. 'Glug-glug-chubble!'

'Watch this, Kyle!' Jade yelled rolling around on the soft cushion of balls.

The toddler wriggled free of Carmel and launched himself at Jade. Soon he was rolling and tumbling, squidging, squirming and totally forgetting to cry.

'Well, that was nice, dears,' Gran said and hour and a half later. The girls had played themselves to a standstill and Kyle was asleep in his push-chair.

'Not!' Kayleigh grumbled. That was ninety minutes when she could have

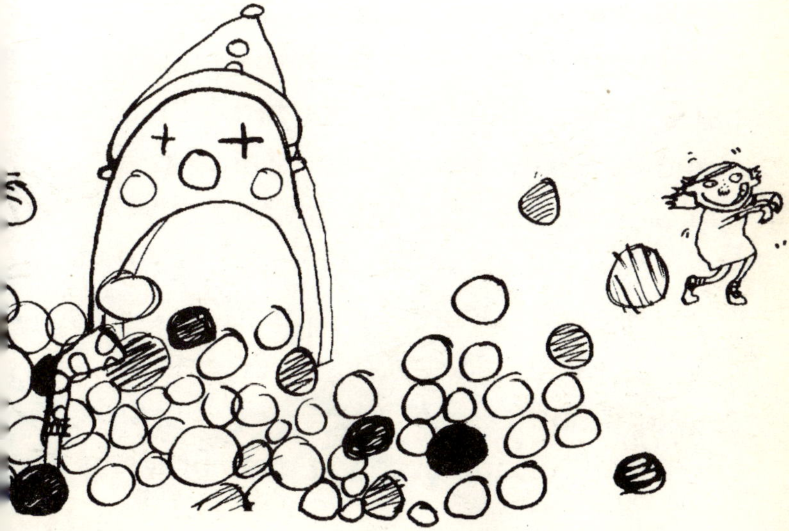

been looking into a mirror, trying out eye-shadows and lip-liners. 'Can we catch the bus, Gran, plee-eease!'

'Yeah, cool!' Jade grinned from ear to ear. 'Thanks, Gran!'

'How come you didn't join us?' Carmel was asking Krystal, who tossed her pony-tail and chose to walk with fashion-victim Kayleigh. Carmel mimed Kayleigh's walk, hips thrust forward, shoulders back, like a model on a catwalk.

'We're too old for Kidz R Us!' Krystal retorted. 'Anyway, Kayleigh's gonna lend me her Wicked Lady Purple nail varnish!'

'Hi there, girls!' a voice said as they reached the exit from the pub car park. It was Jules from Kangaroo Club, standing with her assistant, Sally, at a table, trying to stop the white cloth from blowing off in the wind.

'Nei-eigh!' Deanne whinnied.

'Have you had a good time?' Sally asked the others.

Helpfully Jade grabbed one corner of

the cloth and pinned it down with a collection box full of loose change. 'What's this for?'

'We're raising money for an extension to the playgroup building,' Jules explained. She had a clipboard in her hand with a list of names written down. 'People can put their coppers into the boxes and also sign up for our big event next weekend.'

'Sounds interesting,' Gran smiled, emptying her purse of 2ps and 1ps. 'What's this Big Event you're planning?'

'It's a Fun Run,' Jules told her. 'Next Saturday. Entrants get people to sponsor them, just like in the London Marathon.'

'Cool!' Jade said, anchoring the table cloth with more tins of money.

Huh? What's fun about running? Kayleigh raised her eyebrows in astonishment. She'd rather lie on a Greek beach any day.

'You do it, Gran!' Carmel jiggled her with her elbow. She had a picture in her head of poor Gran struggling up a hill wearing a sweatband around her forehead and baggy tracksuit bottoms.

'Me? Oh no, I'm way past it!' Gran laughed and patted herself on her large chest.

'Rubbish!' Jules argued. 'We've had seventy-year-olds entering; people of all shapes and sizes. It doesn't matter how long you take, so long as you complete the seven miles.'

Seven miles! Kayleigh's mouth fell open. She wouldn't run seven *steps*; not for a million pounds.

'That sounds an awfully long way,' Gran gasped.

'All for a good cause,' Sally reminded her, sensing that she was wavering. 'I'm doing it, and I must be nearly your age.'

'Yeah, Gran!' Carmel said. A little demon had got into her head and made her push her gran forward. Gran in a lycra leotard, training and doing press-ups. '*Sally's* put her name down!'

Gran frowned and ummed and aahed. 'I suppose it would be a good way to lose a few pounds.'

'Yeah!' Krystal encouraged.

'You don't think I could!' Gran accused her smirking grandchildren. 'Well, let me tell you, I won medals in athletics when I was at school. I threw the javelin for my county!'

Javelin? Gran with the big chest? Jade couldn't help it; she bent double and laughed out loud.

'Put my name on that list!' Gran told Jules with an edge of steel in her voice. 'And put Jade down for the junior section. If she can't sit still for two minutes at a time, why not put some of that energy to good use for a change?'

Two

'Wicked!' Carmel cried down the phone to her mum and dad. 'Gran's gonna do the Fun Run! You have to sponsor her.'

Jade grabbed the phone. 'And me! I'm in the junior section. I'm gonna earn loadsa money for the Kangaroo Club!'

'Run that by me again,' Dad said. 'Did I hear Carmel right; your Gran's going to take part in a running race?'

Jade giggled. 'Yeah, she's out training in the garden right now.'

There was a long pause before Dad went on. 'Tell her I'll sponsor her for fifty quid if she makes the full distance.

Otherwise, it'll be a fiver per mile.'

'Cool. How much are you gonna give me?'

'Twenty quid for finishing, or else two quid a mile.'

'Huh, that's not fair! Why should Gran earn more than me?'

'Because she's a gutsy old lady to sign herself up for this, and you're a lively young thing who can do it standing on your head.' Dad stood firm against Jade's indignant whine.

'Huh!' Jade huffed. 'Just because I'm nine I earn less! That's ageist!'

'Well, write to your MP about it. Meanwhile, get some other people to sponsor you,' Dad told her from his sun-lounger in Corfu. 'I'm sure it'll soon add up to a fair amount. Anyway, twenty quid is not to be sniffed at.'

'*If* I finish,' Jade grumbled. Suddenly the thought of joining the Fun Run didn't seem so attractive. 'This is seven miles we're talking about!'

'Here, give me the phone.' Kayleigh stepped in to talk to her mum and dad. 'What's the weather like? How hot is it? Are you brown?'

Jade sagged back on to the sofa in front of the telly, while Carmel joined Krystal at the window. Deanne passed through the room mooing.

'Cow!' the twins acknowledged. Today a cow, yesterday a horse, the day before that a kangaroo.

'Moo!' Deanne lowed gently through the back door, then swayed out into the garden to chew grass.

'Yuck!' Krystal said.

'She's faking it,' Carmel noted. 'She's not really munching. Come here, Kyle. No! Don't eat the grass. It's nasty; yuck!'

Kyle had crawled out after Deanne and seemed to find the grass quite tasty. He stuffed a handful into his mouth and chewed it thoughtfully.

'OK,' Kayleigh said, rounding off her talk with Dad. 'I'll tell Gran you'll sponsor her. Oh and by the way, I'm gonna get my nose pierced on Monday. I know this place that does it. They shoot a gold stud into your nostril with a staple-gun thingy. It doesn't hurt and it looks really cool ...'

'No way,' Dad said, and put down the phone.

'Pants!' Kayleigh sighed.

Out in the garden, Krystal and Carmel were trying to make Kyle spit chewed grass out of his mouth.

'Moo!' Deanne said, picking daisies

and sticking them in her hair.

'Puh!' Krystal taught the baby how to spit. 'Puh-puh!'

Kyle quickly got the hang of it. 'Pu-thhhuh!' Green slime splattered everywhere.

'Gross!' Krystal sprang back and wiped her T-shirt.

'Hey, don't call Gran bad names!' Carmel cried, catching sight of the figure at the bottom of the garden.

'Hup-two-three, hup-two-three!' Gran grunted. She was doing step-aerobics on a garden bench.

'G-g-gran?' Krystal stammered.

'Hup-two-three!' Gran was wearing a baseball cap and a bright pink sweatshirt, purple lycra tights, stripy pink leggings and brand-new trainers.

'Fifty-eight, fifty-nine, sixty!'

The twins ran up to her as she collapsed on the bench. 'You don't look like *you*, Gran!' Carmel giggled.

Catching her breath, Gran looked up.

'I'll have you know these leggings are the height of fashion!'

'Yeah, way back in the olden days!' Krystal told her. 'Where did you get the sad hat?'

'Never you mind!' Consulting a list which she'd pinned to the garden shed, Gran began her next activity. 'Move back. I have to do twenty press-ups and then I'm allowed to take a break.'

'It's not fair, I can't get my nose pierced ...' Sulking big-time, Kayleigh wandered out into the garden. 'I s'pose I could have it done anyway, then when Mum and Dad got back they wouldn't be able to do anything about it, which would serve them right for jetting off to the sun and leaving us with Gran ... Gran???'

Gran lay flat on the grass, face-down, in shiny purple tights and pink leggings. Krystal and Carmel stood watching her.

'Moo!' Deanne murmured, sticking flowers in Kyle's fluffy blonde hair.

'Crazy!' Kayleigh muttered. 'What's going on?' she asked Carmel.

'Gran's training for the Fun Run. She has to do twenty press-ups, but she can't seem to get the hang of it.'

Huff-puff-groan. Gran failed to heave her body clear of the ground. 'Don't just stand there,' she told the girls. 'One of you will have to show me how to do it.'

'Not me!'

'No way!'

'Don't even think about it!'

'Fetch Jade,' Gran insisted,

her face red and sweaty.

So Kayleigh strolled back into the house to fetch the expert. 'Gran wants you to demonstrate some press-ups,' she said casually. 'She's got this list of exercises to get fit for the Fun Run.'

'Easy-peasy!' Jade said scornfully, not lifting a finger. 'Anyone can do press-ups.'

'Yeah, Ms Superwoman. So how come you're not training?'

'I am; look!' Jade demonstrated clicking the TV remote on and off.

'Funny girl – not!'

Just then, the wail of a siren started in the distance and drew closer. *Waah-waah, waah-waah*, an ambulance drew up at the Wildes' garden gate. Two men in green overalls jumped out and burst in on Gran's training programme.

'Stand clear!' the first paramedic shouted, pushing his way between Krystal and Carmel. He saw Gran lying face-down, huffing and puffing.

'It's OK, love, just hang on. We'll soon have you right.'

'Uh-uuhh!' Gran said.

Kayleigh and Jade sprinted down the lawn. 'What happened? Did she have a heart attack?' Kayleigh cried.

The twins looked at each other, dumbstruck. They were as shocked as anyone at the sound of the siren and the arrival of the emergency services.

The paramedic turned Gran's head to one side and felt the pulse in her neck. 'She's having difficulty breathing,' he reported to his mate. Heart rate is way off the top of the scale!'

'Uh!' she said.

'Don't worry, your neighbour saw her collapsed on the grass with a suspected cardiac arrest,' the second man told the girls. 'She dialled 999. We got here as quick as we could.'

'Is Gran gonna die?' Kayleigh whispered shakily.

'Uh-uuuhhh!' Gran protested.

The men talked of clearing airways and using a defibrillator.

'B-b-but!' Carmel found her voice at last.

'She didn't ... she isn't ...' Krystal tried to explain.

Jade crouched beside the patient and listened carefully to what she was saying.

'Stand back!' the paramedics insisted, taking tubes and pads out of their bag.

'Speak up, Gran!' Jade urged.

'I said, leave me alone!' Gran gasped, stranded on the lawn like a fish on a river bank. 'There's nothing wrong with me!'

'She says she's fine,' Jade reported to the two men.

Krystal, Kayleigh and Carmel breathed sighs of relief.

'Great. Now just give us some space to work,' the first one insisted, totally ignoring Jade and moving in to turn

Gran on to her back and insert a tube into her mouth.

Gran coughed and struggled. 'Uh-lee-me-be!'

'She says to leave her be,' Jade translated patiently.

'Look, love, we know what we're doing. You have to let us get on if you want your gran to be OK.' The second man dodged Gran's flailing arm and set about lifting her sweatshirt.

'Oh no you don't!' Gran sat bolt upright, arms across her chest. Her face was cherry-red and shiny, her baseball cap sat crooked on her short blonde hair.

The paramedics fell back, as if a corpse had suddenly come back to life.

Taking a deep breath, Gran straightened her cap and stood up. 'I'd like to say thank you very much for worrying about me and wanting to help,' she told the two men primly. 'But the truth is, I didn't have a heart attack. I'm simply in training for this weekend's fun-run!'

'I've a good mind to wring Maggie Wade's neck!' Gran said darkly over the Sunday roast. 'The whole street was out rubbernecking to see if I was going to pop my clogs in public. When in fact, all that had happened was that I was taking – er – a short break from my training programme. And the next I knew the ambulance came rushing up the street, all because that silly woman poked her nose in!'

The sound of happy scoffing accompanied Gran's complaints. Kyle played the drum on the tray of his high-chair.

'I've been reading this book,' Kayleigh announced.

Krystal and Carmel spluttered in disbelief. 'No! Never! A real book without piccies?'

As they giggled at their own amazing sense of humour, Jade snuck in with a snide remark of her own. 'Hey, Deanne, d'you know what we're eating? It's beef – moo – cow!'

Deanne seemed to ignore her and carried on scoffing.

'Cow! Moo! Steak!' Jade muttered.

'Oink!' Deanne snorted, handing a roast spud to her invisible friend, Buggle-mug.

'What kind of book, Kayleigh?' Gran asked kindly.

'It's about older people training to stay fit. It's called *Fit at Fifty*. I found it on Mum's bookshelf.'

'Yeah, see! I bet it's got millions of piccies!' Carmel crowed.

'That's very nice of you, dear,' Gran said, taking the large, glossy book from Kayleigh and leafing through it. '"*Fit at*

Fifty",' she read. '"By the author of *Healthy at Heart* and *One Hundred and One ways to Unwind.*" Yes, I see, it has an actual programme of exercises, with drawings and diagrams – jogging, weights, cycling, swimming – hmm, I think I'll use this in my own training. Thank you very much!'

'Gran, I was wondering, would you give me some money to have my nose pierced?' Kayleigh asked sweetly.

'What, dear?' Gran turned the pages. 'No, dear. Definitely not.'

'Hah!' Jade jeered.

Kayleigh gave her a death-dealing look. 'Gran, don't you think Jade should start training for next Saturday as well?' she said in a loud voice.

'Hm? It says here that people of – er, shall we say a certain age – should ease gently into exercise and not rush straight into things.'

'Jade should be doing press-ups and weights if she wants to do well,' Kayleigh insisted. 'She can't enter the run without a proper build-up.'

'Since when did you know anything about keep-fit?' Jade asked. 'The only bit of *you* that gets any exercise is your big mouth!'

'Oink!' Deanne said, poking her snout into Kyle's dish of roast potatoes.

Gran glanced up from *Fit at Fifty*. 'Kayleigh's right,' she told Jade. 'It says here that you have to prepare your cardio-vascular system for extreme exertion, and that this applies to everyone, at any age, no matter how fit.'

'Huh?' Carmel asked. 'What's that in plain English?

'It means Jade will conk out if she tries to run seven miles without training,' Krystal explained. 'I agree with Kayleigh and Gran.'

'Me too.' Carmel was happy to gang up against Jade. 'Lots of circuit training, while the rest of us slob about by the open-air pool eating ice creams!'

Jade scowled and sank down in her chair. 'I'm already fit. I don't have to train.' This Fun Run thing was definitely turning out to be a bum idea.

'Yeah, and it says in the book you have to follow a special diet.' Kayleigh was deeply into the theory of getting someone else fit, as long as it didn't endanger her own fingernails and lip-gloss. 'No choccy or sweet things. No ice creams.'

'Yeah!' Krystal and Carmel agreed with bright smiles. Next week was looking Bad with a capital 'B' for Jade.

'Right!' Gran decided. She snapped the book shut as if she meant business. 'No sticky toffee pudding for you and me, Jade!'

'No pudding!' Jade squeaked.

Rat-tat-a-tat-tum! Kyle played the big drum.

Gran went into the kitchen to fetch the steaming pud. 'Who wants custard and who wants cream?' she called.

'Custard!' Carmel yelled back, and Deanne gave an oink.

'Cream!' Kayleigh and Krystal cried. Kyle rattled his spoon.

'Both!' Jade clamoured.

But Gran stuck to her word. She and Jade sat pudding-less as the others scoffed and slurped.

'Tough!' Kayleigh muttered out of the corner of her full mouth. 'But don't worry. Jade, it'll be worth it. Once I've worked out your full training programme you'll be the most mega fit runner in the junior event!'

Three

'First, jog on the spot for fifteen minutes,' Kayleigh instructed.

'Right you are, dear!' Gamely, Gran began the task. *Huff-puff, huff-puff.*

'What's the point of that?' Jade asked. As far as she was concerned, the only reason to run was to get somewhere fast.

Kayleigh told her that it was a good warm-up technique. She had put on a sporty top and combat trousers to look the part of personal fitness trainer. 'Look, are you gonna do what you're told, or not?'

Jade glowered at her audience of Krystal, Carmel and Deanne.

'Go on, it's for a good cause,' Krystal encouraged.

'If you train properly, we'll help with the sponsorship,' Carmel offered.

Jade grunted. 'Does that mean you'll pay me some dosh?'

Straight away Carmel regretted opening her big mouth. 'Erm, maybe. Or maybe we'll go next door and ask Mrs Wade for you.'

Huff-puff. Gran jogged steadily.

Jade thought deeply for a moment. 'OK, listen to this. I'll train if you pay!'

'Out of our own pockets?' Krystal turned pale and clung on to Carmel. 'How much?'

'10p a mile. Or £2 if I finish.'

'No way!' Krystal made an instant decision. 'I'm saving up for a CD!'

'OK,' Carmel said. 'You can have my dosh as long as you put in the proper training.'

Jade narrowed her eyes suspiciously. 'Honest?'

'Yeah, honest!' Carmel promised. It was worth 10p a mile to see Jade suffer for a whole week. No puddings. No ice creams. No choccy.

Huff-puff. 'How many minutes is that?' Gran gasped.

'Three. Still twelve to go.' Kayleigh was keeping her eye on the stopwatch she'd found amongst a clutter of ancient keep-fit equipment in the garage. 'C'mon, Jade, get your ass into gear!'

Deanne spread her wings and flew silently round the garden. She tilted her arms at each corner, flapped, then hovered.

'Eagle,' Kayleigh explained casually.

'Come on, Jade, get it on!' Carmel chanted. 'No gain without pain! Feel the burn!'

So, grunting and chuntering, Jade started to jog.

'Second; ten minutes on the cycling-machine!' Kayleigh didn't even give them a break between exercises.

'Boring!' Jade moaned.

But Gran jumped on and began to pedal.

'OK, while Gran's busy with that, you can try the weights,' Kayleigh hassled. She was really into this fitness training; maybe she would even make a career of it.

'Yeah, skinny ribs. Try the weights!' Carmel was enjoying the show. Gran wobbled while she pedalled. Jade hated every second. 'This is for the kids of Hartsbridge!' Carmel reminded them. 'Put your backs into it!'

So Jade strained and lifted.

'Cor, look at those muscles!' a voice said from behind the hedge.

A startled Jade dropped the weights on her foot. 'Perry Wade!' she cried.

Perry, the boy from next door. *Nightmare!*

'Ignore him,' Kayleigh told her. 'He's always snooping, just like his mum.'

Perry, the geek. Perry, the sneak. Perry, the loudmouth.

'He'll blab to everyone!' Jade groaned, diving for the privet and scrambling through to the other side, where she confronted the spy.

'I'll kill you if you say a single word about this!' she threatened.

Perry pretended to tremble in his size 13s. At nine, he was one of those kids who had never had the chance to be young. Old freckly face; old, dry, crinkly hair; old cracked voice. 'I'm really scared!' he told Jade sarcastically. 'I promise I won't tell anyone that

I've seen your weedy efforts, cross my heart and hope to die.'

'"Cross my heart and hope to die!"' Jade mimicked in a mincing voice. 'I'm warning you, Perry; if the footie gang finds out I'll know who to blame. And believe me, what I do to you won't be pretty!'

Perry raised his fair eyebrows. 'Wow, I'm wetting my pants – not! Hey, I see your Gran's heading for another heart attack.'

*

Kayleigh checked her stopwatch. It was 4.15 pm. Both Gran and Jade had taken turns on the cycling machine and the weights. The twins were stuffing a Snickers bar into Kyle's mouth. Jade was idly circling the lawn, floating on air currents.

'Next; dance aerobics!' Kayleigh announced.

'Oh no, not that!' Jade cried. *Not namby-pamby dance aerobics!*

'Yeah, that is pretty sad,' Krystal agreed.

But Kayleigh was already plugging in her music centre to a long extension lead, wondering how much a professional personal trainer could charge per hour. *I could get rich doing this,* she thought. *I could be trainer to the stars. Pop idols would ring me up and plead for me to train them. Famous Hollywood actors would have to go on a waiting list ...*

'Run to me, baby, run to me, In my

arms you're gonna be free! Run, run, run to me!'

The words of Ziggy Palumbo's latest number one blared out across the lawn.

'Copy me,' Kayleigh told Gran and Jade. 'I'll do one demonstration, then you join in.'

'What was that noise?' Krystal muttered to Carmel. She thought she'd picked up a sound from the Wades' garden.

'Sshh, I'm watching Jade's face!' Carmel giggled.

'Left foot forward, left foot back, sidestep with the right!' Kayleigh sang out, demonstrating her disco technique.

Gran bobbed about, waving her arms and jigging.

Jade stood with a face like thunder.

'Do it!' Kayleigh barked. 'Sidestep to the left, kick with the right!'

Jade jerked to the right and kicked with the left.

'Tee-hee!' someone snickered from behind the hedge.

'Stay with me, ba-aby, stay with me, This love of ours is meant to be! Stay, stay, stay with me!'

'Step forward, step back, quarter-turn to the left.' Stylish Kayleigh showed them how it was done.

Jade stepped back, forward and quarter-turned to the right.

'You're facing the wrong way!' Kayleigh said crossly. 'Look at Gran; she got it right.'

'Ha-ha-ha! Phhh! Sssshhh-hu-ha-ha-ha!'

This time Jade heard the muffled explosion of laughter from Perry's garden. She froze in horror then tucked her chin into her chest and strode across.

'Sidestep left, sidestep right!' Kayleigh went on, trying to ignore the interruption.

'I'm gonna kill you, Perry Wade!'

Jade cried, ducking through the gap. She came face to face with ... Perry, Mark, James, Danny, Bo and Jez.

The boys rolled about with tears in their eyes. They guffawed and giggled, choked and chortled.

Perry had only gone and blabbed to the whole five-a-side football team, that was all!

'Left, right, turn around!' Danny gulped.

'Jade Wilde's got two left feet!' Jez cawed.

Jade saw red. She launched herself at Perry and grabbed him by the throat. He got her back with a judo throw to the ground. She looked up in surprise. How come geeky Perry knew judo?

'Fight!' the boys cried.

Krystal and Carmel piled through the privet hedge and waded in on Jade's side. Mark tried a karate kick on Carmel but landed on his back. Krystal got in first with a head-butt against Bo.

'Just you wait!' Jade warned Black Belt Perry. She lunged forward with a kickbox to the chest.

'Stop!' Mrs Wade came trotting down the path, wielding an egg-whisk in her right hand. She'd been making meringues for Sunday tea when she looked out and saw the fight. Now she began beating children instead of egg whites. 'Take that, you nasty girl!' *Whop-whop!* 'Let go of my Perry!'

The whisk did the trick, and soon the Wildes retreated to their own garden.

'Two steps forward, two steps back, half-turn to the right!' Kayleigh and Gran had carried on regardless.

'What am I gonna do?' Jade wailed. 'It'll be all over the park that I was doing a stupid dance!'

'Yeah, and you were really pants at it,' Krystal sympathized.

'I'll kill 'im!' was all Jade could say, while Deanne beat her wings silently and Gran did a twirl.

Kayleigh consulted her training programme. Monday morning meant more weight lifting and the start of road work, building up to sit-ups and stretching exercises before a short break for lunch.

'Morning!' Krystal stuck her head around Jade's bedroom door.

'Uh-uh!' Jade groaned from under the duvet.

'It's a mega sunny day. We're off to the pool!'

Jade flung back the duvet and sat up. Her hair looked like a bird's nest. 'Wait for me!' she cried. 'I'm coming too.'

'Sorry, not possible,' Carmel reminded her. 'Kayleigh's the boss, and she says you and Gran have to stay and train.'

'Uuhh!' Jade sank back.

'Get up, lazy-bones!' Gran appeared, dressed and raring to go in a tent T-shirt and the purple lycra. She jogged on the spot, one-two, one-two!

'Which swimmie d'you want to take?' Krystal called to Carmel from the top landing. 'The lime-green one or the stripey one?'

'Stripey!' Carmel answered, zipping off to find two beach towels.

'Make that three,' Krystal yelled. 'Deanne's just said she wants to come too.'

Deanne wandered up the stairs, waving one arm in front of her like a trunk and trumpeting quietly.

'Elephant,' Kayleigh commented, coming into the room and seeing Jade still in bed. 'You've got five minutes to get dressed and come outside,' she barked. 'This is Monday, remember; only five days to go!'

Jade buried her head and had dark thoughts. *I could put Kayleigh out of action with one of those weights ... one quick thump, and then no more lousy training ... hmm, perhaps not. Run away? Where to? Fake an injury? ... Hmmm.*

'Bye!' Five minutes later, Krystal and Carmel barged by Jade's bedroom

door, armed with beach bags and their inflatable shark.

'Hey!' Carmel dashed in and ripped the duvet off Jade. 'C'mon, get up! Kayleigh's waiting!'

'I can't!' Jade wailed. 'I've sprained my ankle – look!'

Carmel stared at the huge bandage wrapped around her sister's leg and foot. 'Since when?'

'Since yesterday, when I dropped that weight on my foot. It swelled up like a balloon while I was asleep!'

'Yeah; like, I'm supposed to believe that!' Carmel sniffed.

'She's faking it,' Krystal agreed.

'I'm not. Fetch Gran!' Jade groaned, doing a good impression of a soldier dying on the battlefield. Luckily no one had seen her nip into the bathroom to grab the crepe bandage and a handful of cotton wool to pad it out with. 'I don't think I can train for the Fun Run any more,' she sobbed weakly.

Real tears.

'Oh, poor dear!' Gran said when she came up from the garden in her baseball cap and shades and saw Jade clutching her poorly leg with her cheeks all wet. 'You must've overdone it.'

Jade checked a sly grin. 'It really, really hurts!' she groaned.

In the background, Kayleigh eyed her suspiciously. 'Let's leave her,' she told Gran. 'We've got loads of stuff to get through.'

'Are you sure you'll be all right?' Gran fussed, gingerly prodding the bandage.

'Ouch!' Jade yelped. 'Yes, I'll be fine,' she said through gritted teeth.

'Should we call the doctor? Or perhaps take you to the hospital for an X-ray?'

'No!' Jade squeaked. Maybe she'd overdone the yelping a teensy weensy bit. 'It'll be OK if I rest it.'

Kayleigh, Krystal and Carmel tutted and snorted, but Gran fell for it. 'You lie quietly and read a book,' she suggested. 'Kayleigh and I will be out in the garden. If you need anything, give us a shout.'

By ten-thirty the sun was blazing down and Kayleigh's schedule called for a short break. 'Fifteen minutes!' she ordered, ticking boxes and checking her watch.

'The pounds must be falling off me,' Gran gasped, with sweat dripping down her face.

'Orange juice, but no biscuits,' Kayleigh told her.

'Which reminds me; we haven't heard a sound from Jade's room lately!' Gran declared, planning to sneak a custard cream from the box on her way through the kitchen. 'I must go and check!'

A custard cream and a ginger nut. What harm could two measly biscuits do? Gran snaffled them and crept upstairs. *Munch-munch.* 'Jade, dear, I've brought you some orange juice and biscuits!'

There was no reply, so Gran eased open Jade's door. 'Asleep,' she murmured, setting down the glass and biting into Jade's chocolate digestive.

'What's going on?' Kayleigh had followed Gran and stared in at the shape covered by the duvet.

Gran gulped and swallowed guiltily. 'Nothing, dear. Jade's gone back to sleep.'

Frowning, Kayleigh came closer. She inspected the hump and was about to prod it when Gran interrupted.

'Don't do that; it'll wake her, poor lamb.'

Kayleigh hesitated, but only for a nano-second. Then she pounced and dragged back the duvet. 'Yeah; poor *lamb*!' she cried.

The hump was two pillows laid end to end.

'Oh!' Gran gasped. Then, 'The little monkey!'

'Typical!' Kayleigh spat out. 'But if Jade Wilde thinks she's gonna get out of training for the Fun Run, she's definitely got another think coming!'

Four

Krystal, Carmel and Deanne played all day.

They whooshed down the water-slide and frolicked in the fountain. For lunch they bought Cheesy Wotsits and ice cream. All afternoon they dived and swam.

'Cool!' Krystal sighed, examining her sunburned shoulders. 'I've got strap-marks!'

'And freckles!' Carmel told her, just to annoy her.

'Have not!'

'Have!'

Deanne the Dolphin made funny little creaking noises.

'Let's go!' Krystal rolled up her wet towel and threw away her empty bottle of sun cream. The sun was going down and the pool was emptying.

'One more dive from the top board,' Carmel insisted, legging it to the deep end. She climbed then stood poised, arms raised, looking down at the clear blue water.

'Carmel, phone call!' Krystal yelled, holding up her mobile phone.

Carmel jerked, overbalanced and plunged headfirst. *Smack!* She belly-flopped from a great height.

'Only kidding!' Krystal giggled when Carmel dragged herself out of the water.

So the twins weren't speaking as they made their way home, and the Dolphin had gone quiet too, until they came to the park and she began nudging and creaking again.

'Leave it out, Deanne!' Carmel complained, elbowing her away.

'Aa-a-a-aak!' Deanne squeaked excitedly, pointing her flipper towards the footballers in the park.

'Yeah, quit it, Deanne,' Krystal echoed, in no mood to play her weird sister's game.

So Deanne plopped over the wall and swam across the grass. 'Aa-a-a-ak!' she called from the edge of the makeshift football pitch.

'Tutt. What's she on about now?' Grudgingly Carmel looked. She squinted, blinked, then looked again. 'Jade?' she muttered.

'Jade ... what?' Krystal was confused. Surely Jade was at home in bed, resting her sprained ankle – ha ha! But no; when Krystal followed Carmel over the wall and trotted to join Deanne, she saw Jade tackle Danny, take the ball, run with it past Jez then blast it past Perry in goal.

'Jade!' Krystal and Carmel gasped.

Goal! Their injured sister sprang into the air, then slid down on to her knees, arms outstretched to receive the fans' adoring cheer.

Bo scooped up the ball and trotted by close enough for Krystal to collar him. 'How long has Jade been down here playing footie?'

'All day. She's scored five. We're winning 12-9!'

Carmel frowned then stormed on to the pitch. 'You're meant to be training!' she yelled at Jade.

Jade grinned and hopped about. 'Can't. My ankle kills!'

'Step to the left, step to the right, kick and turn!' Perry minced. The other boys fell about laughing.

Jade bopped the nearest one, who happened to be Mark. 'I'm not doin' that stuff any more; right!'

'You have to!' Krystal insisted. 'Kayleigh's in charge of your training programme. She's gonna kill you when she finds out about this.'

'Don't care.' Jade sniffed. She'd made up her mind. 'Whatever she says, I'm never gonna do that stupid aerobics ever again!'

'We've been so worried about you!' Gran told Jade when the twins dragged her back home. 'Ever since eleven o'clock this morning, I've been wondering where you were!'

'It's called facing the music!' Krystal had insisted, pushing Jade from behind.

'Yeah; meeting your responsibilities,' Carmel had agreed, dragging her from the front.

They'd manhandled her all the way from the park and dumped her in front of Gran and Kayleigh.

'Gran was worried but *I* wasn't,' Kayleigh snapped now. 'I knew you'd been faking that sprained ankle all along!'

'What are you gonna do to her?' Carmel demanded. 'You know she's been playing footie in the park all day!'

'Dirty rotten grasser!' Jade muttered.

'We dobbed you in for your own good,' Krystal argued. 'You need to be in proper training for Saturday.'

'Who says?' Jade had been dragged home all muddy and scuffed after her day of scoring goals and being mobbed by the fans. She'd had a cool time, and now she didn't care what happened to her.

'*I* say!' Kayleigh glowered. 'It tells you in the book.'

'Yeah, *Fit at Fifty*,' Jade sniffed. 'That's for wrinklies, not for me.'

'Er-hum!' Gran coughed, pulling in her stomach muscles and sticking out her chest. 'Less of that, thank you.'

Jade shrugged. 'Sorry, Gran, but I'm not doing it. I'm not doing the dance stuff, or the weights, or anything.'

'What?' Kayleigh fizzed and fumed. 'Huh! Typical! Coward ... chicken!'

'You think you can boss us about, just because you're the oldest and Mum and Dad aren't here!' Jade challenged. 'As a matter of fact it's all your fault that I had to sneak off this morning. If it hadn't been for you, I'd never've had to do it!'

There was a flaw to this argument that Kayleigh wasn't quick enough to pin down. Instead she huffed and puffed and came to the boil. 'You listen to me, Jade Wilde! I'm sick of you. I've decided I don't want to be your personal trainer any more!'

'Good!' Jade snapped. ''Cos I'm not doing it anyway!'

'Good!' Turning her back, Kayleigh crossed Jade off her schedule.

'Listen, I don't mind running and stuff, but I'm not into all this training.' Jade tried to explain to Gran. 'And the same about Saturday; I don't want everyone like Jez and Bo and Perry staring at me at the start, saying, "Hey, Jade's running with the grannies!" and laughing and all that.' After all, it had just taken her a whole day and scoring five goals to get back in with the footie gang.

'You won't be running with the grannies,' Krystal pointed out. 'You'll be in the junior section.'

Jade sagged. 'Yeah, with the five-year-olds. How sad is that!' Head hanging and mumbling awkwardly, she came out with what she really felt. 'I never wanted to do this Fun Run in the first place.'

'You have to now!' Carmel cried.

'Yeah, you can't back out!' Krystal

chimed in. 'I've already been and got five sponsors for you. '

'Plus Mum and Dad,' Carmel reminded her.

Deanne creaked and crept alongside Jade. 'Ak-ak,' she said gently.

'Would you do it if you didn't have to train with Kayleigh?' Gran asked, her voice full of concern. She ignored Kayleigh's harumphing snort and came close to Jade.

Jade sighed. 'The thing is, it wasn't my idea,' she told Gran quietly.

'No, it was mine. I press-ganged you into it because you'd giggled about me throwing the javelin, I seem to remember.'

Jade blushed. 'Yeah, sorry.'

Gran glanced down at her big chest. 'I can't really blame you, can I? But in my day I was a little whippet of a thing, just like you. And don't you look at me like that, Miss Krystal!'

'Wha? Whuh?' Krystal pleaded

innocence, but it was no good; Gran had seen the smirk.

Gran gazed at each of the girls; at Deanne creaking softly, Kayleigh frowning, Carmel and Krystal hiding their grins behind their hands, and Jade looking tired, dishevelled and desperate.

Then she took Jade's sponsor sheet from the table, held it up and tore it in half. 'You're right,' she told Jade. She tore it into quarters. 'No one can force you. You don't have to do the Fun Run if you don't want to.'

She ripped the sheet into tiny white pieces and they all watched in amazement as they fluttered gently to the floor.

Jade was off the no choccy and ice cream regime. She could come and go as she pleased. So she went. As far away from the others as possible.

'I can't say I'm not disappointed,' Gran confessed on the Monday morning, staring at Jade's empty chair. She'd just taken Kyle to Kangaroo Club and told Jules that Jade had backed out of the charity event. 'The playgroup needs to raise an awful lot of money for this extension. They have a waiting list as long as your arm and are desperate for more funds.'

Krystal munched her honey-nut corn-flakes. 'Jade never does stuff she doesn't like. I'm telling you, if it doesn't involve a ball, you might as well forget it.'

'Don't eat with your mouth open,' Carmel reminded her.

'Hah!' Krystal was about to flick a soggy cornflake at her sister until Gran frowned at her.

'I suppose it's down to me,' Gran sighed, putting on her cap and flexing her aching muscles. 'I'd better get out there and train!'

'... Thirty-eight, thirty-nine, forty!' Kayleigh counted.

Gran finished her sit-ups and collapsed in a heap.

'... Faster!' Kayleigh commanded.

Gran pedalled on the exercise bike until her face ran with sweat.

'... Ten more laps!' Kayleigh cried.

Gran staggered on round the park in her purple leggings.

'Poor Gran!' Carmel said as she lazed by the river. 'Last night Kayleigh even stopped her from watching telly and sent her to bed early.'

'Yeah, and look at Jade now.' Krystal pointed to the group of kids splashing and fooling about in the shallows. Jade was in the thick of it, organizing a game of water-basketball.

Jog-jog; Gran ran past the twins. 'It's time to pick up Kyle!' she gasped. *Jog-jog.* 'Would you two go and collect him?' *Jog-jog.*

So Carmel and Krystal wandered off through the town, stopping to admire the glittery hair bobbles in Boots then counting their change to work out if they had enough money for a bag of chips from the Fish Dish. They arrived at the playgroup with greasy fingers, five minutes late as usual.

'Look who's here, Kyle!' Jules announced to the only toddler left in the empty room.

Kyle saw the twins and scuttled away under a yellow plastic chair.

'Gotcha!' Sally said, picking him up and handing him over.

Carmel and Krystal were about to beat a hasty retreat when Jules stopped them with, 'It's a pity about Jade and the Fun Run.'

'Yeah,' they nodded. *Don't give eye contact. Pretend you have to dash.*

'What happened? Did she get injured?' Jules asked.

'Yes!' Krystal said. *Quick, we're out of here!*

'No!' Carmel contradicted.

Jules frowned. 'Yes or no?'

'Not exactly,' Carmel admitted. 'She just went off the idea.'

Jules's silence made them both squirm.

('There we were, feeling guilty because you'd backed out!' Krystal told Jade later.)

'Gan-gan!' Kyle said, looking round for Gran. When he didn't see her waiting at the door he began to bawl.

'She won't change her mind,' Krystal explained above the racket. 'Gran knows that. She even ripped up Jade's form.'

Jules nodded, locking eyes with them and sighing.

('That was where we went wrong,' Carmel pointed out in bed that night. 'We gave her eye contact!')

Krystal shuffled from foot to foot, while Carmel tried to quieten Kyle with a squished Rolo she'd found in her pocket.

'I don't suppose there's any point asking either of you to do the Fun Run instead?' Jules asked quietly.

Krystal hummed and Carmel haahed.

'No way,' Krystal muttered. Then she weakened. 'Oh well, give us a sponsorship form just in case.'

Sally whipped one out of her overall pocket. 'Good for you!' she grinned.

Krystal took the form. 'I'm not saying I will,' she warned, thinking of the no-telly and early nights involved. 'Not for definite.'

'Take the form anyway,' Jules

encouraged, smiling at her. 'You're a good, kind girl, Carmel!'

'I'm Krystal,' Krystal pointed out, then kicked herself. The mistake had just given her a cool idea.

'Whatever. Go and get as many sponsors as you can!' Closing the door behind them, Jules went off in a more hopeful mood.

'Gan-gan!' Kyle wept, as if he would never see his gran again. Tears rolled and snot ran.

Carmel joggled him. 'I can't believe you just did that!' she told Krystal.

'What?' Krystal pressed the button for the green man and waited patiently.

'That! You just volunteered for the Fun Run!' Krystal was almost as bad as Kayleigh about exercise. She hated getting out of breath and messing up her hair.

'Didn't!'

'Did!' Carmel had seen it with her own eyes. Krystal offering to step in for

Jade. Well, practically. OK, she'd said maybe not for definite. But as good as. Carmel was gobsmacked.

The green man said 'Cross'. Krystal marched ahead of Carmel and Kyle. She strode on through town without a single glance at the hair-straighteners or the styling gels.

'What's going on?' Carmel demanded as they reached the park. 'How come you just volunteered?'

Krystal stopped and turned. 'You don't get it, do you?'

'Get what?' Carmel backed away as Krystal waved the rolled-up sponsorship form under her nose.

Krystal smiled. This was where her cool idea came in. So cool and so clever that no way would Carmel be able to say no: 'I didn't volunteer *me*, silly. I volunteered *you*!'

Five

'No!' Carmel bellowed. 'N-O-No!'

She shouted so loud that Jade broke off from her footie and raced across. 'What happened?' she cried.

'Krystal wants me to do the Fun Run instead of you!' Carmel roared. 'It's all your fault for backing out!'

'Whoah!' Jade stepped back. 'Don't tell me. I don't wanna know!' Quickly she sped back to the important business of scoring goals.

'What's wrong, dear?' Gran asked, jogging lightly by.

'Three more laps!' Kayleigh instructed,

her eyes on her stopwatch.

'Tell Krystal she can't make me!' Carmel pleaded, running alongside her gran.

'Can't make you do what, dear?' There was a spring in Gran's step. It seemed that all this training was paying off.

'Run in the Fun Run instead of Jade!' Carmel bleated.

'What a good idea!' Gran beamed, deliberately misunderstanding and leaving Carmel stranded at the foot of a hill.

Already Krystal was going around the park collecting sponsors for her twin. 'Jez, sign this. How much can you afford? I'll put you down for 5p a mile. Bo, how about you? You're loaded; you can pay 10p!'

The boys signed so that they could concentrate on the footie game; even Perry. 'I'll do 50p a mile!' he boasted.

'Wow, Perry, did you win the Lotto?'

Krystal made him sign before he could change his mind.

He snorted. 'No way. But Carmel's a couch-potato. She'll never make the full seven miles. Maybe one or two at most, then she'll be dead!'

'I'll tell her you said that, Perry,' Krystal warned.

'Don't bother, I heard him!' Carmel had stormed across and tried to snatch the form off Krystal. 'Anyway, no need to worry; I'm not doing it!'

'You so are!' Krystal argued.

'I'm so not!'

'Girls!' Gran sped by, light on her toes. 'Let's talk about this later.'

'What's to talk about?' Carmel sulked over her spaghetti. 'I said no, didn't I?'

'But I promised Jules!' Krystal whined. This was it; the point where her cool, clever plan would come in!

'You promised her that *you'd* do it, remember!'

'But she was well confused. Maybe she still thought I was you! Everyone knows you're better at running than me.'

Carmel felt the whole family following their argument like spectators at a tennis match; heads this way, then that. 'But you're the oldest,' she muttered.

'Yeah, by a puny ten minutes. What difference does that make?'

'Gran, tell her!' Carmel pleaded.

Suck-suck! Strands of spaghetti

disappeared into Kyle's round mouth like worms down a hole. Red sauce dribbled down his chin.

'What am I supposed to say?' Gran sighed. 'First Jade lets the side down, and now you, Carmel. It's beginning to look like I'll be the only person in this family with enough decency to line up at the start tape on Saturday!'

'Buggle-mug will do it!' Deanne chirped.

'Oh yeah, like we'll get millions of sponsors to sign up for the invisible boy!' Kayleigh scoffed.

After that there was silence. Long, heavy, awkward, empty.

Slurp! Kyle sucked his pasta.

Guilt! It settled like lead in Carmel's stomach, turning her yummy spaghetti into a plateful of pap. She pushed it away and leaned both elbows on the table.

Silence.

'I thought I could rely on at least one

of you to keep me company in the race,' Gran said.

Kayleigh busied herself with tomorrow's schedule, while Krystal checked through Carmel's sponsors. (The guilt thing was definitely working on Carmel, just like she'd known it would.) Jade experimented to see if she could press her thumb against the wrist of the same hand. Deanne's bottom lip wobbled as she explained silently to Buggle-mug why he would not be taking part in the Fun Run.

Boy, did Gran know how to come down heavy on a person! Carmel bit the inside of her cheek, waiting for one of the others to weaken first.

Kayleigh studied her fingernails, Krystal wound spaghetti around her fork, Jade jiggled her feet against her chair legs, Deanne sniffled.

'Oh OK, I'll do it!' Carmel groaned.

'Yeah! Whoo-ee! Cool!' The cry went up.

Krystal relaxed. *Perfect!*

Gran smiled and whipped Kyle out of his chair. 'Bath-time!' she announced, taking the stairs two at a time like a twenty year-old.

'Support the Kangaroo Club!' Krystal shouted from the fountain at the top of the High Street. It was Tuesday; the first day of Kayleigh's emergency campaign to get Carmel into shape.

The night before, Gran had zipped along on the sewing-machine and whipped up an amazing kangaroo suit for Deanne to wear. It was made of fawn fur-fabric, with long ears, long tail and a pouch.

'Sign with Skippy!' Krystal begged the passers-by. 'Give Hartsbridge a pre-school centre to be proud of!'

Deanne hopped here and there, *beh-doing!* She presented Carmel's sponsorship list to the estate agent, the butcher and the girl from Boots.

'Good job!' the Big Issue seller told Kayleigh. 'You can come and work my pitch if you like!'

By the end of the day, Krystal and Deanne had collected fifty-three names and addresses.

'That comes to £103.50!' Krystal announced over supper. She'd done the maths with the help of a calculator, adding up the 5 and 10ps per mile. 'But only if you go the whole distance, Carmel!'

'Uh-uh-uh!' Pressure, pressure! Carmel was flat-out on the sofa after a day of press-ups, sit-ups, aerobics, cycling, jogging. Every inch of her body ached.

'Feel the pain! Burn baby, burn!' Jade muttered.

'Ha ha!' Carmel hardly had the energy to reply.

'Never mind, you'll feel better by Day three,' Gran told her, zipping along on her sewing-machine once more. She was sewing ear-shaped pieces of silver fabric on to what looked like a head-band.

'What're you making?' Krystal asked.

'Wait and see,' Gran replied, merrily trilling the words to an old song; 'Will you still need me ... rrrrr ... Will you still feed me ... rrrr ... When I'm sixty-four!'

'It's-for-the-good-of-the-playgroup!' Carmel gritted her teeth and went the extra mile. It was Wednesday; she'd given up all treats and dedicated herself to the cause. 'If I'm gonna do this, I'd better do it properly!'

But not the dance stuff. Like Jade before her, she drew the line at that. As she said to Krystal, 'No way am I poncing about in front of Perry Wade!'

Jade ran to the hedge where she knew Perry was watching through his spy-hole. 'Did you hear that? Carmel just called you a ponce!' she called.

Perry grunted then lobbed over a lump of dry earth. It landed on Kayleigh.

'Beware enemy missile!' Jade cried, diving flat on her face and crawling commando-style for the house to answer the phone.

When she picked it up she heard a fuzzy crackle then her dad's voice saying strange stuff, something like 'Kalimera' and 'Ti kanes, pethaki mou?'

'What're you on about?' Jade demanded over the crackles.

'Kalimera – good morning. It's Greek. Ti kanes, pethaki mou – how are you, my darling?'

The sun seemed to have gone to his

head. Either that, or he'd been drinking.

'Cut it out, Dad,' an embarrassed Jade muttered.

'No, I mean it. How are you all?'

'Fine.'

'How's your gran doing with her training?'

'Fine.'

'How many eggs in a bakers' dozen?'

'Fine ... come again?'

'See, I knew you weren't paying attention. Am I going to get anything other than "fine" out of you?'

'Sorry.' Jade was glancing out of the window at Kayleigh shaking earth out of her hair then darting through the hedge to pummel Perry. Meanwhile, Gran and Carmel were lifting their weights.

'What's the score with your own preparations?' Dad asked against the hiss of the poor line.

'Sorry, can't hear you,' Jade lied. She changed the subject fast. 'Listen, Dad, Gran's made Deanne a cute kangaroo costume, and Kayleigh says she's gonna be a personal trainer to the stars.'

'I take it your training isn't going too well?' shrewd Dad guessed. 'Jade, I hope you're taking this fund-raising thing seriously. Your mum and I want you to support the Kangaroo Club as much as you can.'

'Yeah,' Jade mumbled.

'So do your best, OK.'

'Yeah.'

'And don't sound so glum!'

'Yeah. I mean no.' This was *so* not cool! 'Bye!' she said, slamming down the phone.

'I've given up everything I love for this Fun Run!' Carmel sighed. They'd got through Thursday and she was lying awake in bed, still aching, talking to the cracks in the ceiling. 'This is supposed to be the summer holidays and I can't go swimming, or eat pudding, or watch telly. Kayleigh's a

slave-driver, and everything's pants!'

'I heard that!' Kayleigh screeched from her room next door. She'd been checking what she thought might be a zit on her nose.

'I don't care. That's what you are; a slave-driver. Even Jade couldn't hack it!' Carmel grumbled. 'And no one in this family is tougher than Jade.'

'Gran can hack it!' Kayleigh retorted, coming through and plonking herself on Krystal's empty bed. 'Anyway, all the books say you have to go through a pain barrier when you work out. It's called pushing your envelope.'

'I don't wanna push my stupid envelope.' Carmel groaned as she sat up. Even her stupid-stomach stupid-muscles hurt!

'You'll thank me in the end,' Kayleigh told her, perched there in her denim jacket and boot-legs, hair swept up in a high ponytail.

'No I won't!'

'Yeah, well someone has to do it. Listen, Carmel, I think I've got a talent for this personal training. I mean, I'm really into it. What d'you think?'

'Yeah, you're a slave-driver,' Carmel confirmed. It was no surprise to her that her oldest sister had turned into a monster. 'You should join the army and yell at new recruits. Or else be a teacher.'

'Ha ha!' Catching sight of herself in the wardrobe mirror, Kayleigh stood up and gave a twirl. 'You can buy some really cool clothes for the gym. I'm gonna save up. Eventually, maybe next year, I'll start running fitness classes. Then I'll take on clients and give them one-to-one lessons.'

Carmel gave a hollow laugh. 'Dream on! People won't pay you real money to make them feel as bad as I do!'

'Yeah, they will. They do this stuff all the time in America, and now it's big over here too. Anyway, how come you agreed to do it if you hate it this much?'

''Cos!' Carmel said with a frown.

''Cos – what?'

''Cos Krystal made me feel such a louse!' G-U-I-L-T! It was called GUILT! It sat on your stomach until you gave in.

Kayleigh stood up with a swing of her ponytail. 'That's your trouble,' she told Carmel. 'You're way too nice!'

Friday dawned with storm clouds in the sky.

'Never mind,' Gran said. 'The forecast says it'll clear up by tomorrow.'

Make it rain! Carmel pleaded silently.

We want thunder and lightning. Let all the trees fall across the road and big floods come, so that we can't do the Fun Run!

'Today we're going to try out the actual course of the race,' Kayleigh announced. She was zipped up inside an orange cagoule, to keep out the big splodges of rain that had begun to fall.

'What, *all* of it?' Carmel squeaked.

'Yes, and I'll be with you every step of the way to make sure you don't cheat,' Kayleigh assured her, showing her the bike she would ride alongside as Gran and Carmel ran.

'Come on, let's go!' Gran said, leaving instructions for Krystal and Deanne to take Kyle to Kangaroo Club and then collect him at lunchtime. 'Oh, and check with Jules that it's OK for us to wear fancy dress tomorrow!'

'Gan-gan!' Kyle wailed when he saw that she was leaving.

Splosh! The rain hit the pavement in giant drops. The clouds swept low over the hills.

'We'll head for the swimming pool,' Kayleigh instructed. 'That's the official start of the run.'

Splosh-splosh. Slowly at first the rain came down, then faster, until by the time they reached the pool, the roads were standing in puddles.

Splat-splash! Carmel's trainers slapped into the water. Thunder rumbled in the sky. 'Do we *have* to do this?' she wailed.

'Wuss!' Kayleigh said, putting up an umbrella and steering her bike with one hand.

Ducks came up from the river bank and waddled through the puddles. A flash of lightning forked through the sky.

'Eek!' Kayleigh cried, her umbrella turned inside-out by the wind. 'Head for the swimming pool entrance. Run for it!'

'So we waited by the chocolate machine until the lightning stopped,' Carmel reported to Deanne, Krystal and Jade. 'I snuck a Mars bar when Kayleigh wasn't looking! Then Gran said she thought we'd better come home in case anyone else was scared of lightning. For once Kayleigh didn't argue. And here we are.'

Kyle hadn't gone to Kangaroo Club because of the storm, so they were all gathered around the telly with mugs of hot chocolate.

'Did I die and go to heaven?' Carmel sighed, lying back on the sofa and toasting her feet on the radiator. For the first time in ages she was allowed to relax.

Then Gran came in, hiding something behind her back. 'I've got a surprise for you, Carmel,' she twinkled.

Another treat? Wow, this was one cool day! Carmel sprang to her feet to see what it was.

'Hold it. It's your costume for tomorrow,' Gran said. 'I have one to match.'

Costume? Since when? Carmel hesitated and bit her lip.

'We'll look the same!' Gran promised. 'I thought it would be nice to have a giggle.'

'What is it?' Carmel asked, feeling the dread descend.

'First the ears and the tail!' Gran

held up a pair of silver rabbit ears and a round ball of cotton wool. 'And now the T-shirts!'

Carmel grabbed the black top and read the silver letters across the chest. Bootilicious Bunnies! 'What are we meant to be?' she gasped.

'It's obvious, isn't it?' Gran beamed.

'No, it isn't!' Carmel stammered.

Gran laughed at her horrified stare. 'Get with it; we're Bunny Girls. Bootilicious Bunnies! What d'you think?'

Six

Dear Krystal,

I've been through the pain but I can't stand the shame! Gran forcing me to be a Bunny Girl is one step too far. Please tell Jules I'm sorry I've let her down, and try to make her understand.

By the time you wake up I'll be long gone. No way can they make me wear the ears!

Love from your twin sister,
Carmel xx

PS Don't try to find me.

Krystal stood in her pyjamas. She read the letter three times with shaking hands before she could bring herself to tell the others.

Carmel must have snuck out at dawn, before anyone was up. Her trainers were gone from under her bed and her jim-jams were flung into a corner. The note had been propped against Krystal's stuffed penguin on the mantelpiece, written in turquoise felt-tip on lilac paper, in a place where it couldn't be overlooked.

Krystal took a deep breath and crept downstairs to Jade's room. 'Carmel's bunked off!' she told her.

'Ha ha!' Jade moaned from under her crumpled duvet.

'No, she has! Here's the note. Read it.' Thrusting the paper under the cover, Krystal plonked herself on the end of Jade's bed.

Jade rubbed her eyes and read the message. She emerged from her bedclothes with a wide-eyed stare. 'Wicked!' she gasped. One of her sisters had actually, in real life, no kidding, run away!

'You have to tell Gran,' Krystal told her.

Jade shook her head, bounded out of bed and ran to Deanne. 'Read this! Carmel's skived off the Fun Run!' she hissed.

Deanne snuffed and huffed like a sleepy hamster. She read the wobbly turquoise writing. 'Why doesn't Carmel want to be a bunny?' she asked.

'Because she'll look stupid, stupid!' Jade said, snatching the note back. 'You'll have to tell Gran, Deanne!'

'Not me!' Deanne shook her head, and quicker than you would have believed (for a hamster) grabbed the note back again. Then she ran upstairs to Kayleigh's room, pursued by Jade and Krystal.

'Do Not Disturb!' said the notice on

Kayleigh's door. It was locked from the inside.

Deanne lay flat on the floor and hissed under the door. 'Kayleigh, wake up! Carmel's scarpered!'

The door flew open and Kayleigh stood there in her nightie and a green face-mask. 'Wha-d'ya 'ean, Car'el's scar'ered?' she asked without moving her lips.

'I mean, she's run away. She isn't here. She's not gonna do the Fun Run!' Deanne insisted.

'Isn't it wicked!' Jade gasped.

'Typical!' Krystal frowned. 'Trust Carmel to spoil everything!'

'Not gonna do the 'Un Run?' Kayleigh echoed through the stiff paste. Only her eyes, nostrils and lips showed. She spoke through clenched teeth, like a ventriloquist's dummy.

'She couldn't stand the shame,' Jade explained. 'It was the ears that did it!'

Kayleigh's eyes darted from one to the other.

'She's gonna hide until it's all over,' Krystal went on.

'She says not to try to find her,' Deanne added. 'Someone's got to tell Gran!'

'Tell Gran what?' Gran called, coming out of the bathroom with Kyle.

'Nothing!' came the chorus from the top landing.

Kyle turned a tin of baby talc upside down and shook it over the carpet.

'This is so not 'air!' Kayleigh spluttered, crying tears of frustration over her green mask.

'So not what?' Jade asked.

''Air!' Sob-sob.

'Fair!' Krystal interpreted. 'Sshh! Wait till Gran's gone downstairs!'

'Aachoo!' Gran breathed in the baby talc. 'Will somebody tell Carmel it's time to get up!' she called after her as she carried Kyle downstairs.

The girls grimaced from the top floor.

'*You* tell her!' Krystal urged Kayleigh, who was wiping off the green gunge with a swab of cotton-wool.

'No, *you* tell her, Jade!' Kayleigh sniffled.

'*You* tell her!' Jade said to Krystal.

'We've been through all this,' Krystal sighed. 'I know; let's just *not* tell her!'

'Huh?' Jade didn't get it.

'Let's go and look for her instead!'

'But she said not to,' Deanne pointed out.

'Since when did we take any notice of what Carmel says?' Kayleigh quickly agreed Krystal's plan. 'The thing is, we have to find her and get her to the start line, whatever it takes!'

Jade nodded. 'Cool!'

Kayleigh was coming round from her

blubbing session. She grabbed Krystal by both shoulders. 'And for now, you put on Carmel's T-shirt and shorts and pretend to be her!'

Krystal tried to back away. 'You must be nuts! What for?'

'So Gran doesn't know she's scarpered!' Kayleigh explained. 'As far as Gran's concerned, there's no panic, see? Which gives us time to sneak off and find the real Carmel!'

'Cool!' Jade and Deanne hissed. 'Do it, Krystal!'

'I dunno – this gives me a bad feeling!' Krystal sighed and shook her head.

But Jade dived into the twins' room and dragged Carmel's stripey T-shirt out of a drawer. 'Stick it on!' she insisted. 'We'll pretend we're going out to collect more sponsors before breakfast, and we'll say you, Krystal, went on ahead, so then you can act like Carmel, as if you've just got up. It's easy-peasy!'

Reluctantly Krystal agreed.

'Waaagh!' Kyle wailed hungrily from the kitchen, beating his spoon on his plastic tray.

'Let's do it!' Kayleigh insisted. 'We've gotta find Carmel if it kills us!'

'Where would *you* hide?' Kayleigh asked Krystal.

They'd fooled Gran into thinking that they were raising more money for the Run. 'I've got butterflies in my stomach,' she'd confessed to Krystal, who was pretending to be Carmel. 'I don't know about you, dear, but I'm really feeling quite nervous about today!'

'Me too,' Krystal had answered, and she hadn't been lying.

Now Kayleigh was pinning her down with the question about where Carmel would hide. 'Why ask me?' she protested.

''Cos you're her twin, so you think like her,' Kayleigh reasoned. 'You've got the same kind of brain.'

OK, so where would she choose?

'Somewhere quiet, where no one goes. Somewhere no one would expect. Oh, and somewhere where there was food.'

Kayleigh, Jade and Deanne thought about this for a while.

'How important is the food thing?' Jade asked.

'Mega.' Krystal sounded sure. 'Especially chocolate.'

'So we should head for the shops?' Kayleigh asked. They were gathered outside the Fish Dish, trying to decide their tactics. The clock above the Building Society said half-past eight.

'No, too crowded,' Krystal said.

'How about the pool?' Jade suggested. 'There's a choccy machine by the ticket office. And there are loads of changing cubicles for her to hide in.'

Krystal nodded. 'Let's split up. Me and Jade can head for the park and the pool. You and Deanne can try Woollies and the 8 Til Late, just in case.'

Kayleigh agreed. 'Meet back here in half an hour. And listen, look as hard as you can, 'cos if we don't find her, we're dead!'

'That's it, then; we're dead!' Krystal sighed.

She and Jade had scooted through the park, asking Mark and Bo if they'd seen Carmel.

'Sorry,' Mark had shook his head and Bo had booted the ball between the goal posts. The girls had left them scrapping in the dust and trotted on to the pool.

'No, sorry,' the woman on the ticket desk had told them. She had been busy re-filling the chocolate machine when Krystal and Jade had sprinted in. 'We're not open yet, so there's no way your sister could've come through the barrier.'

Jade had frowned. 'Carmel might've snuck through.'

'Not with me standing here,' the

Guardian of the Gate had insisted fiercely. Like, it would be instant death if anyone had tried.

'Couldn't we just *look*?' Krystal had pleaded, straining to see beyond the desk into the changing-room and the outdoor pool beyond.

The blonde woman had turned on them with her fake tan and tight Ellesse top. 'No, you could not!' she'd snapped. 'You're not the first to use the excuse of looking for a friend in order to blag your way in without paying, and you won't be the last!'

So Jade and Krystal had retreated and made do with skirting the tall hedge surrounding the pool. They'd peered through the shiny laurel leaves at the still, bright blue

expanse of water, noting that the fountain was switched off and the slide deserted.

'Hang on, I won't be long!' Jade had told Krystal. Fearlessly she'd climbed a nearby beech tree and swung along an overhanging branch until she could launch herself over the hedge and on to the grass surrounding the pool.

'How're you gonna get back out?' Krystal had hissed.

'You wait here for five minutes, then go back to the ticket place and make a big fuss about something.'

'About what? Krystal pleaded.

'I dunno. Use your imagination. Give me time to sneak out while the woman isn't looking!' Jade had given her instructions then scooted off to check the changing rooms. She'd tiptoed in, holding her nose at the sharp smell of chlorine, peered into every cubicle and found no sign of Carmel; not one wet footprint or a single Snickers wrapper.

So she'd hightailed it to the exit, to find Krystal explaining to the blonde bouncer that she was sure she'd seen an object floating in the deep end. 'I thought it was just rubbish,' she had been gabbling, 'but then I looked again and saw it was a big black dog. Yeah, definitely; there's a dog swimming in the pool!'

The woman had tried to laugh it off, but she'd glanced nervously over her shoulder. 'If you're having me on ... !' she'd threatened, stomping off to take a proper look.

'Nice one!' Jade had vaulted the barrier and joined Krystal. They'd scarpered again before the dreaded, fire-breathing Guardian had returned.

But when Krystal learned that the secret search hadn't turned up a single clue, her heart sank. 'We're definitely dead,' she repeated, as she and Jade headed up to the Fish Dish to meet Kayleigh and Deanne.

*

'Stick with me!' Big Sis told Deanne. 'I don't want you being a giraffe and going off on safari!'

Deanne tucked herself in beside Kayleigh. She still didn't understand the bunny problem, but she could tell the situation was urgent.

'After all my hard work,' Kayleigh complained as they searched the Woollies sweet counters, 'Carmel has to go and ruin everything!'

She marched up to the cash desk and asked the assistant if they'd seen a girl with shoulder-length, dark brown hair buying a stack of chocolate.

'Yeah,' the kid with the cash grunted. 'Hundreds of 'em.'

And that was all he would say.

The same in 8 Til Late, and in the newsagents, and the same from the Big Issue seller, who would definitely have helped them if he could.

Kayleigh and Deanne scoured the

whole town until they came to the Kangaroo Club.

'Hi, girls!' Jules called from the top step. She was carrying stacking plastic chairs out to her van, ready to drive stuff across to the start of the Run. Sally was following with a load of brightly coloured flags. 'How's your gran? Is she ready to go?'

'Yep!' Kayleigh assured her.

'And Carmel?' Jules staggered past with her load.

'Er – yeah,' Kayleigh answered uneasily.

As the door swung to behind Sally, Deanne nipped inside for a quick go on the ball slide. Hey, she hadn't done this since she was three! Wow, it was fu-un ... wheee!

Deanne landed in a swirl of balls and sat for a moment. Was that a noise from the playgroup kitchen? A mousy, secret little noise? Maybe she should go and investigate.

So Deanne tiptoed across the room and peered around the door. Nope; there was nothing to see.

But then there was another noise, like a tin lid rattling on to the floor.

'Rats!' a voice said from inside the cupboard.

'Eek!' Deanne sneaked, snuffling the air and creeping forward. She opened the cupboard door. By her ears and whiskers, she'd been right!

'Deanne!' Carmel gasped with a mouthful of choccy biscuit. She was

crouched inside the low, dark cupboard, clutching a big tin of Chocolate Assorted.

'Eek!' Miss Mouse squeaked.

'I was hungry!' Carmel said guiltily. 'I didn't have any money with me, and the door was open, and I knew there'd be something to eat, and anyway it was a good place to hide!'

Deanne listened and stared.

'Don't dob me in, please!' Carmel begged. 'I don't want to be a Bunny Girl!'

'Deanne?' Kayleigh yelled from the front door.

'Plee-eease!' Carmel begged.

Deanne closed the cupboard door and trotted to meet Kayleigh.

'Stop messing around,' Kayleigh said crossly, closing the door and stomping down the steps.

Deanne eeked and twitched her ears and whiskers, thinking about Carmel hiding in the cupboard. But she said nothing.

'That's it; we're dead!' Kayleigh sighed, glancing at her watch. It was time to meet Jade and Krystal, then to go home empty-handed and tell Gran that her fellow Bunny Girl and highly trained running companion had - well - erm - done a runner!

Seven

'Carmel, thank heavens you're back!' Gran cried, grabbing Krystal before anyone had time to say a word. She was pacing up and down the hallway in her silver ears. 'I was beginning to think that you'd let me down too and I would have to set off for the start of the Fun Run all alone!'

Plonk! Krystal felt the clamp of the Bunny Girl alice-band around her head. The hall mirror showed her with a pair of glittery ears and a shocked expression. 'I'm – I'm ...' she stammered.

'Yes, yes, I know. But there's no time

to say sorry!' Gran hustled her through into the kitchen. 'Put this T-shirt on and velcro this bunny tail on to your backside.' *Whisk! Zap!* 'That's right. Now we can go!'

'B-b-but!' Krystal murmured. She stared down dismally at the Bootilicious Bunnies logo on her chest.

'Wicked!' Kayleigh cried, peeking through the door. 'Wow, *Carmel*, you look really groovy!'

Krystal turned on her with a savage stare.

'Yeah, *Carmel*, you're well cool!' Jade assured her. No way was she, Jade, gonna break the bad news to Gran that Carmel wasn't who she seemed. Life sometimes played a perfect trick, and this was definitely one of them.

'Come on!' Gran ordered. 'I've left Kyle with Maggie Wade next door. Everything's organized, and I'm raring to go!' One-two, one-two! Gran jogged on the spot.

'Help!' Krystal hissed to Kayleigh, Jade and Deanne. 'Get me out of this!'

But her scummy sisters kept quiet and pushed her out of the front door after Gran.

'Good luck, *Carmel*!' Jade yelled.

'And don't forget everything I taught you!' Kayleigh added with a sweet smile.

Gran hauled Krystal down the path and out on to the street. 'I've still got those butterflies in my stomach!' she gasped. 'More like a bag full of ferrets, actually. All those people are gathered at the start of the race, and the Kangaroo Club is relying on us! Why, I haven't been so nervous since – since I queued up for Cliff Richard's autograph!'

Deanne, Kayleigh and Jade watched their ears bob up and down along the top of the hedge.

'Phew!' Kayleigh sighed. 'Nice one!'

'Yeah. Let's just hope that Krystal doesn't chicken out at the last minute,' Jade muttered. Then they fell quiet while Deanne trotted down the path to watch Gran and Krystal's back view of waggling ears and bobbing white tails.

'I wish *I* had silver bunny ears,' she sighed.

The sun shone on the start of the Fun Run. The puddles of the day before had dried out and conditions were perfect for the one hundred and fifty runners.

'Aren't we lucky with the weather?' Jules greeted each contestant with a smile and then pinned a number on their backs.

Gran and Krystal lined up alongside Bob the Builder and Mickey Mouse. In the background, tiny tots from Kangaroo Club sang 'The Wheels on the Bus Go Round and Round' while their mums rattled collection tins.

How on earth did this happen? Krystal wondered. *I mean, how?*

Gran waved at her friends in the crowd. 'Ooh-hoo, Maureen! Ooh-hoo, Lesley! It's me, Sylvia! Who'd have thought I'd ever get roped in for this, hey?'

Maureen and Lesley had dropped by on their way home from shopping. 'We're gobsmacked! Put us down for a fiver!' they called back.

'The wipers on the bus, Go swish-swish-swish!' the tots belted out.

Krystal's mouth was dry, her heart thumping. 'I'm – I'm – I'm not ... !' she began. But she couldn't finish. How could she drop Gran in it, now, at the very last moment? Then again, how could she run all those miles after the second helpings of pud and half a ton of chips that she'd eaten so far this holiday? She looked ahead at the hill that rose up behind the swimming pool. Whoah, no way!

'The bell on the bus, Goes ding-a-ling-ling!' the kids yelled.

Three dads in proper running gear lined up at the start, beside the Bootilicious Bunnies. They flexed and stretched their muscles and took deep breaths. 'Five minutes to go!' one muttered.

Red and blue flags fluttered in the breeze, Jules smiled and pinned on more numbers.

'Pity the other girls didn't come along to lend their support,' Gran sighed, glancing at the throng of spectators. 'Never mind, Carmel, you and I are going to show them how it's done!'

Krystal's tongue stuck to the top of her mouth. The hill rose up before her, and she wished with all her heart that she could undo all the hours spent slobbing on the sofa. Her silver ears wobbled.

'Quiet, everyone!' Jules called in her

playgroup leader voice. 'Would all the runners line up at the start. Remember, there are refreshment tables at the side of the road at regular intervals along the route for you to take on water or juice. A St John's Ambulance crew is standing by. All I need to do now is wish you the best of luck!'

Help! Krystal squeaked. *I can't do this! Way too many crisps and choccies!*

There was a huge jostle of runners. Bob the Builder squashed up against a cowboy in a white stetson, Mickey Mouse stood on Elton John's toe.

'Can I come too?' a quiet voice said to Gran.

Gran looked down at Deanne dressed in last Christmas's Rudolph the Reindeer horns.

'I'm a deer,' she explained, looking up with her huge brown eyes. 'Deers can run fast!'

Gran smiled. 'You *are* a dear!' she agreed, taking her hand and squeezing

it. 'Of course you can come. And if you can't keep up with the grown-ups, one of the nice helpers at the refreshment tables will look after you.'

'Ready?' Jules cried above the hustle.

Deanne took her place in between Gran and Krystal.

'Shove over!' Jade joggled Krystal to one side. 'Make room for me. I'm coming too!'

Krystal's mouth fell open. 'Is this for real?' she gasped. 'Or am I gonna wake up in a sec and find it was all a dream?'

'Quit it!' Jade muttered, limbering

up beside the serious dads. 'I couldn't very well let you conk out halfway up that hill without a back-up Wilde sister to run the rest of the race, could I?'

'Get it on, Jade!' came a loud shout from the crowd. Perry Wade led Mark, James, Danny, Bo and Jez in a mini Mexican wave.

'Jade!' Gran turned and beamed. 'I knew you'd have a change of heart, and here you are!'

Jade blushed, gritted her teeth and glared at Perry. 'You're dead!' she mouthed.

'... Steady!' Jules yelled.

The crowd of runners parted and Kayleigh came through, glammed up as usual in her slinky strappy top and silky jogging bottoms.

'*What?*' she said to an open-mouthed Krystal. She tossed her ponytail. 'Listen, it's no big thing. I'm just here to make sure *someone* from our family makes it through the finish tape, that's all!'

'Whatever!' Jade growled. 'You never even ran for a bus, remember!'

'Just watch me!' Kayleigh replied, clenching her fists.

'Nice to see you, dear,' Gran smiled, as if nothing could surprise her any more. *One-two, one-two!* She ran on the spot, waiting for the final word.

'... Go!' Jules thundered.

And just at that moment Carmel barged between Bob and Elton, using her sharp elbows to arrive beside Krystal, pale and mussed-up but grimly determined.

'Don't look at me like that!' she warned, lurching forward with the crowd of runners. 'I'm here 'cos I felt bad about leaving that note, OK! I mean, BAD bad – pain in the stomach, can't stay away bad!'

'And they're off!' Jules cried.

Cameras flashed, the crowd cheered.

Past the church at the top of the hill, through the bluebell woods, past the posh white houses and back down into the valley, the Wilde sisters ran.

FUN RUN
Bootilicous
Bunnies!